What the Heart Holds Safe

a Delta Force romance story
by
M. L. Buchman

Buchman Bookworks

Other works by M.L. Buchman

The Me and Elsie Chronicles

Newsletter signup at:
www.mlbuchman.com

1

The round that took out the US Army Ranger behind D.K. "Deek" Davies passed less than six inches from his ear. Not worth even noting except for the harsh supersonic *snap* as the bullet rushed by. Then the Ranger collapsed against him which screwed up his next shot, sending it high and to the right. Guy shouldn't have been hovering so close that he collapsed forward when hit.

Deek shrugged, the Ranger slid off his shoulder and collapsed to the ground.

"Shit!"

It was Jimmy Borman. His eye was gone,

blood dripping through the squeezed-tight eyelid, the other eye staring wide. A straight-in brain shot. Going home in a box.

"Shit!"

Jimmy had no more home that he did. Certainly not one to go back to.

Deek forced his breath to steady and put his eye back to the sniper scope.

"Shit!" Not Jimmy. Please. It couldn't—

Deek had a shooter out there that he had to stay focused on so he didn't allow himself to look down and confirm what he'd already seen. All he knew was that this goddamn Libyan sniper was going to go down and go down hard.

The question was, where had he gone?

The target couldn't be dumb enough to stay in the same spot as his last shot, but Deek had to check anyway. Nope. Now he'd have to wait for their sniper to try for someone else before…

"Brand, get up here."

While he was waiting for his fellow Delta Force operator to belly crawl across the roof from where he lay with the rest of the Ranger protection squad, he did look down. And cursed himself for doing so. He'd been thrilled to see Jimmy after eight years—the closest Deek ever had to a childhood friend. Embedded one fucking month and…this. Deek reached over and flipped open Borman's heart pocket—the left breast pocket of his inner vest. (For now he'd just think of him as Borman. Keep the wall up, at least until this was done.) No letter, just the slick feel of a photo. Deek tugged it out to see who he'd left behind. Guy was real close-mouthed about whether or not he had a girl.

Deek had meant for it to be just a quick peek, praying there wouldn't be a photo with kids. There wasn't. It was Jimmy's sister Cindy—so stunningly blond and happy. Oh Christ! If there was ever a woman he didn't want to see again it was her. No such luck. It would be up to him to make The Call. Then the obligatory visit next time he was state-side. Some decent act—and that was a whole lot of suck. So much for keeping the fucking wall up.

Brand crawled up beside Borman, three more Rangers were hunkered down covering his six (making sure no one snuck up behind him while he was focusing on bagging the sniper out there). Brand started to roll Jimmy over.

"Too late for him." Deek tucked Cindy's photo into his own pocket and ignored Brand's watchful gaze. He and Jimmy went way back, as far as Deek ever cared to remember, but there was no time to feel now. That was for later. Focus.

"Get his helmet and his rifle. Pop it up over that." He nodded at a stretch of stone banister along the far end of the rooftop. "Duck and weave. Make it look quick but not too smart."

When the helmet came free they both looked away to avoid seeing the bloody mess their friend had become. Borman had been tasked as Deek's close-quarters protection while Deek was doing his countersniper gig and concentrating farther afield. Deek had been looking forward to recommending him for the next Delta testing cycle because the kid had made himself just that damn good. Not so much now.

Deek went back to the scope of his Tac-50 rifle and watched. A slow sweep of the general area. Still no movement. If he were an ISIS shooter— No! Don't stereotype. If his opponent was a smart sniper instead of some dumb kid with a gun, the shooter would be headed…west. Get under the setting sun to blind Deek. It might work, if the sun were half an hour lower, but it wasn't.

Valuing his fingers, Brand had jammed a knife into the bloody padding at the back of Borman's helmet. He eased the helmet up, until barely visible over the wall, then pulled it back down.

Deek shifted his attention west. Maybe behind the tall planter…or the elephant statue. Libya was thick with ornate rooftop ornamentation, much of it riddled with bullet holes from Gaddafi's fall and the disaster that had wracked the country ever since. Rooftop gardens, once the private sanctuaries of the rich and powerful, were now shredded sniper havens.

In his peripheral vision he could see Brand shifting Borman's helmet sideways instead of ducking back down before moving. Then he eased the barrel of Borman's M4 rifle up over the wall.

The sniper's muzzle flash was less than two meters from where Deek had finally centered his scope. He shifted right, compensated an extra half mil mark for the afternoon breeze. Nine hundred meters. His sniper scope was zeroed at a thousand, close enough. In less than half a second, he had the first of three planned shots winging toward the sniper: round one if he stayed put...

Deek heard the *crack* of the sniper's bullet passing by him—farther away this time—as he unleashed his second round.

Round two if the sniper stood up from his shot...

The incoming missed the decoy helmet and splatted on the wall of the building behind them, now just another new divot in the concrete. *Get sloppy when you rush, Mr. Shooter.* Also not smart enough to send two bullets.

Deek stayed steady, waited an extra heartbeat, and fired the last one.

...and round three if the sniper continued moving to the west.

The sniper rose to a low crouch, Deek's first shot—after point-four seconds of travel time—caught him in the abdomen. The second in the jaw. And he must have been tensed to jump to the west, because he managed a single stumbling step forward. His spotter rose to steady him and instead caught the slightly delayed third shot in the head—the two of them collapsed out of sight. The Tac-50's half-inch rounds delivered enough energy, even at nine hundred yards, that neither of them were getting up ever again. Just like Borman.

He and Brand waited fifteen minutes, but no one else took the helmet bait that they tried twice more. The sniper had been potshotting the Parliamentary Building all day yesterday, taking out two representatives and a guard, as if the new government didn't have enough problems in this clusterfuck of a country. Now at least *this* bastard was done with that shit, forever.

Between them they carried Borman (Borman, not Jimmy, getting that wall back up) down the three flights, letting the Rangers take the lead. Normally the Rangers would carry their own and Deek would have let them. But even if they hadn't seen each other in eight years, this was Jimmy Borman and they had a history. He'd been there for Jimmy when he was a screwed up teen, and he was here for him now. Deek sat beside him when they piled into the pair of battered Kia Cerato sedans that had brought them here.

They hauled Jimmy into the safe house and slid him into a body bag. No embedded reporters here, so at least his death would have that much peace. He'd go down as a "training accident" in some other theater, because it was a public "fact" that Delta was not currently operating in Libya.

Now, finally, Deek could let himself feel. Could take time to remember. He'd liked Jimmy, ever since he was the obnoxious kid down the block always tagging after his big sister. He'd had "feisty little shit" down cold then. Eight years later, when he showed up as six-one of badass Army Ranger, he still had it down cold.

Somewhere along the way, he'd taken to tagging after Deek, two lost loners in teenage hell. And again this last month when their units joined up for a little housecleaning in one of the worst countries on the globe. Jimmy had eaten up everything Deek could tell him about Delta. He'd gone from scrawny shit to one tough dude; he said it came from following in Deek's tracks, which was kind of cool.

They'd taken to exchanging hard punches and shouting, "Kick-ass bros!" whenever they headed out on a mission. Damn! Never again.

They slid Jimmy into the cool cellar until they could move him out under cover of darkness. When had little shit Jimmy Borman gotten so damn heavy?

And why did the one thin photograph in his pocket weigh ten times more?

2

Cindy felt the man standing at the door to her office before she saw him. She instantly hit a hotkey to secure the military data and lock her screen before she turned. And then wished she hadn't looked—wished she wasn't in Africa at all.

Sergeant Derek Kyle Davies stood exactly on the threshold of her doorway, looking just as upset to be here as she was to have him here. The eight years since she'd last seen him had barely changed him at all. He was a little broader of shoulder and a little darker of expression, but she'd know him anywhere.

She suspected that his years in Delta Force had done nothing to improve his limited range of expressive grunts.

Perfect.

That meant it was up to her. As usual.

"Hey, Deek." She was the one who'd tagged him back in high school. The silent shadow boy who'd moved in with his drunk of a dad for the last two years of school after his drug-addict mom had walked in front of a train somewhere out west. *Welcome to the South Bronx, sucker. Welcome to hell.* Her first words to him, her only words for a long time. He'd said nothing back, just watched her with that same unwavering scrutiny that he watched her with now.

He took a step over the threshold, then stepped back.

"Goddamn it, Deek. Get your ass in here and sit down," she waved at the folding steel chair beside her desk. Her office was just one in a long line of six-by-eight windowless plywood boxes each with an air vent. Hers was distinguished by a Xeroxed picture of the President the prior tenant had pinned up, complete with an evil Snidely Whiplash handlebar mustache and top hat, that she hadn't bothered to take down.

He finally cleared the threshold, inspected the four walls as if it was a trap about to spring shut on him, then stepped to the chair. He spun it around with a kick and sat on it backwards, resting his crossed arms on the seat back. His presence in her doorway had filled the small room. Now the geometry was placing him much too close to her.

She wondered if waiting him out was worth the effort. He looked like hell, in both meanings. He'd always been handsome as hell, which was all the more powerful because he never leveraged it. The closer girls flocked, the more he retreated. If there'd been a Loners Club back in school, she, Deek, and her brother would have ruled it.

He also looked sadder than she'd ever seen him. Which—

"Oh no! You're here about my Jimmy, aren't you?"

Deek nodded once but didn't speak.

"He's been dead two months. I saw the action report," she snapped a close-bitten nail against her computer screen, "before my commander brought the damned Chaplin in. What the hell took you so long? I'm not that hard to find."

She was a forward operations controller for North Africa Special Operations. Her posting at Camp Lemonnier, Djibouti, Horn of Africa—the only permanent US military base on the whole continent—made her damned easy to find. Deek must have been through here a half dozen times since that operation.

That operation. Her job was coordinating information flow for Special Operations teams assigned to AFRICOM—the US military's unified combatant command for all of Africa. She was the one who had placed the team on that roof. She hadn't issued the order, but she'd chosen the roof, mapped the access points, even arranged for their cars. Though she hadn't known which specific people went until the KIA list showed up at the end of the action report.

Sergeant James Borman. Killed in action (classified).

She hadn't even known until this moment that Deek had been there. In retrospect she supposed that it made perfect sense. Jimmy had been so excited the last time she saw him, assigned to work with Derek Davies after not seeing him once in the years since graduation—Deek had taken his diploma down to the Times Square recruiting station and signed up that day.

And now he must be hurting as badly as she was. Maybe that explained the two months.

He fished into the left breast pocket of his camo jacket and pulled out a piece of paper. No, a photograph. He held it out by a corner trapped between the tips of two fingers. The office was so small that neither of them had to reach far for her to take it.

It was a picture of her, one that had been folded in half. She unfolded the other half though she already knew what she'd see.

Derek.

Making a goofy smile for the camera. No, for Jimmy, who was taking the photo. It was the only time that she'd ever seen him smile happily, and she'd only seen this one in the photo—not in real life.

She closed her eyes to block out Deek's bright smile of ten years ago and the dark and steady gaze of the top Delta Force sniper sitting across from her today. She hadn't cried at the news. She'd refused to cry. It was enough of a surprise that he hadn't died in high school— the South Bronx was a dangerous as hell place to grow up. Even more for a boy like Jimmy. He'd made it out, mostly due to Deek. And done well, until—

A hand took hers, shocking her into opening her eyes and staring at Deek.

"He didn't do anything wrong. Not one damned thing," Deek's voice was no more than a soft growl.

Cindy searched for something neutral to say, some way through the pain that ripped at her heart—an organ she'd carefully isolated and buried long ago. Especially around Deek.

"He was my guard. Sniper caught him. Single round from an unexpected angle. Damned good shot." He grunted the last as a grudging compliment.

Cindy clawed for a breath and managed to gasp out, "Did you get him?" Even though she knew it from the action report, she needed to know, to hear it. Now. From Deek's own mouth.

Deek nodded. "Him. And his spotter."

"Good!" It was all she could manage. She wished Deek would let go of her hand because she didn't have enough willpower to remove it on her own. The warm comfort was both sustaining her and battering down the walls of defense that an abusive father had helped her build. Abuse that she'd accepted in order to protect her little brother from further humiliation. It had continued all through her childhood and teens until one day it had suddenly stopped and he'd never touched her again. Nor had he gone back to abusing Jimmy. Somehow, they were suddenly free.

"That photo," he nodded down toward her other hand. "It's all he had on him."

"Never was much for writing letters or even e-mails," she managed, then looked down at the photo to look away from Deek. "That was a good day."

And it had been. The three of them had taken the D-train all the way down to Central Park and spent the day pretending they were high-rollers. Riding the carousel. Eating ice cream as they walked through the Central Park Zoo. Watching the rich people race their model sailboats on the "Conservatory

Water"—that name had made them all laugh, as if it was too important to be called a pond.

Jimmy had gotten the camera so close in their faces that she and Deek had to crowd together and there was no room for the background around the edges. She could still remember how Deek's hand had felt tight around her waist. He was still the only man ever whose touch didn't give her at least a brief jolt of the creeps. Nobody was as safe to be around as Derek Davies.

"I remember every single minute," Deek's dark eyes studied her closely. Then he raised a hand and brushed her hair back in a soft caress.

For a moment she was lost in it, the breathtaking gentleness from such a hard man. The warm brush of his fingertips as he tucked her hair around the back of her ear. She could—

3

"Don't!" Cindy's snapped command had Deek jerking back his fingers as if they'd been burned.

"What? What did I do?"

"Nothing," but her arms were clenched so tightly about her chest he was afraid she would shatter. "Just don't touch me like that."

"Okay." But he'd always wanted to touch her like that. He'd only ever held her once, that single moment captured in Jimmy's damned photograph. It was the day he'd taken them to Central Park to celebrate—the day after he'd convinced their father that there were worse things than dying if he ever touched either of his children again.

All the women he'd ever been with, he'd ended up wishing they were Cindy Borman instead. Not one of them had been able to purge her wholly from his thoughts.

She was the standard that no one could ever live up to.

When he'd learned the strength she'd had, what she'd done to protect her brother, he'd been utterly humbled. That was the moment he'd fallen in love. Dopey-ass word, but it was the only one that fit. She'd gone from being the only girl he was friends with, to his personal definition of righteous strength.

Ever since then, he'd done his best to match her standard, though no way was he ever going to pull that off.

Sitting here in her plywood cube in boots, camo pants, and tan t-shirt, he'd never seen anything so incredible. He'd watched her work for five, maybe ten minutes before she'd noticed him. He had barely been able to breathe during that entire time. Her blond hair, no longer in a Jennifer Aniston shoulder-length style, was breathtaking chopped off at jaw-level. It was more…her. Her blue eyes now watched him, wide with…fear?

"What is it?"

She just shook her head, leaving him no guide signs for what to say next. He reached out and took her hand again, peeling it free from where it clenched her other arm. She wasn't fighting him, it was just as if she couldn't let go. He clamped her fine fingers between his two hands. He could feel her pulse racing where his finger lay against the inside of her wrist.

"Breathe, Cind."

"Can't!" It was a hard gasp.

"C'mon," he coaxed her. "You pass out on me and we're going to have a situation on our hands. I'm a shooter not a medic. I was so crappy I barely made it through the training." Combat first aid was a part of every Delta's training. He didn't need to have gone for the extra year of medic training to see that she was panicking. Even if he didn't have a damned clue why.

She nodded in agreement but didn't relax. Had she been holding the hurt of Jimmy's loss inside her all this time? Closest thing he'd ever had to a little brother; it hurt like hell. She must be feeling it times ten.

At a loss, he just held onto her hand, imagining he was driving heat into it, though how her fingers could be so cold in the scorching summer of Djibouti he didn't know. It was over a hundred outside and the air-con vent was a joke.

"I really miss the little shit."

She barked out a laugh which was closer to a breath. "He really loved you."

Deek nodded, at a loss for what else to do. The big brother worship had been clear and he'd ended up liking it despite himself. He'd protected both of them when they were kids, and had been cool playing Delta Big Brother to Little Brother Ranger for that month before Jimmy went down. They never talked about the past—except one mention that Cindy was with AFRICOM at Camp Lemonnier—but Jimmy was an easy guy to be around. Deek had liked keeping a protective eye on him—right until the moment he'd fucked up and let Jimmy die.

He knew that wasn't true. The sniper had been well trained. Good enough that they'd sent in a Delta team to clear him out.

So it only felt like it was his fault that Jimmy had gone down, even though he knew—and the mission review team agreed—that it wasn't.

He closed his eyes and raised Cindy's hand to press his cheek against the back of it. Even if it was just for a moment, he had to feel her touching him. For one little instant, he'd believe that it was somehow possible that—

"What are you doing?" She yanked her hand free.

She'd never let him touch her, except that one fine day.

He stood up. Right. Nothing here for him.

He braced himself in the doorway, but didn't turn to look at her when he spoke.

"I'm sorry I couldn't protect him better."

"If he died with you at his side, at least he was happy."

"Uh-huh," he couldn't make the next step off the threshold. He knew if he walked away from Cindy now, he'd never be able to face her again.

But—

"Wait. What?" He looked back at her over his shoulder, still holding onto the doorframe. A battered metal desk, a big computer screen, and the most beautiful woman who could never be his.

"He loved you so much."

"You said that already."

"It's true."

Deek thought about that for a moment. "Guess I loved him too."

"You guess?" Her sadness flashed into fury as she jolted to her feet and strode the three steps to face him.

He turned and looked down at her. Not far. He'd forgotten how tall she was for a woman. Five ten of powerful soldier.

"You guess!" Her fair complexion was turning a mean red. He'd also forgotten that she had a temper—nothing ever phased her brother. He'd go quiet sometimes, but that was all. Cindy? Never any doubt what she was feeling. The only question was—would it hurt.

Apparently a shrug wasn't the right answer as she pummeled the side of her fist against his chest.

"Derek!" No one used his full name. It sounded foreign, even from Cindy.

"He…" Deek started to shrug again then

thought better of it. "Jimmy was the best little brother anybody could want."

"I'm talking about *you,* not me," Cindy's voice sounded as if she was trying to talk to a dumb child and he didn't much like it.

"He was like a little brother to me too."

4

"He was..." Cindy stumbled over the words and almost tripped into Deek's chest. "He loved you."

"You keep saying that. I know it already. I'm not some dumb Jarhead. I'm Delta."

Cindy could only stare up at him, "Jimmy *loved* you, Deek."

"I know that!" His voice lowered dangerously.

"Oh my god," she stumbled back from Deek's dark frown. "He never told you. But I assumed you were—"

"Never told me what?"

No. This could *not* have landed in her lap to do. It wasn't fair. It wasn't possible. If her brother was still alive, she'd kill him. Right here. Right now.

"Cind?" He'd followed her back into the room though she didn't recall retreating until she'd collapsed back into her chair once more.

"Jimmy…was never interested in women. And there was only one man that he ever loved."

Deek blinked twice, then dropped into his own chair, facing her once more.

She waited. To be a Delta Operator meant that he was damned smart. A different kind of intelligence than hers maybe, not one that earned straight As in boring high school classes and everything else since then, but damned sharp.

"Oh shit!" It took him less than five seconds. "He never told me."

"You're seriously telling me that you didn't know?"

His abrupt laugh snapped out like a slap to the face. "He's not my type, Cind."

"Then who is?"

Deek's thin sheen of humor switched off

as if it had never been. His dark eyes stared straight at her. Being a man of few words, he slowly raised one finger and pointed it at the center of her chest.

5

Deek continued his killer workout all through the hot afternoon. The obstacle course was busy with a whole team of swabbies getting their land-side workout and he didn't want to have to eat their dust—something the whole damned country specialized in. Instead he'd eat his own. Delta often fought solo, and he was fine sweating solo. Nobody pushed an operator harder than himself.

Besides, he needed to be alone and do some serious thinking.

He found a tractor tire no one else was using along the back fence of the Special Ops compound and set up a workout. Fifty flips of the five hundred pound tire. Then a hundred agility hops into and onto the tire—first both feet, then right foot only, then left only, coming to a stable stop in each position. Then fifty crunches, sitting on one edge of the tire with his feet hooked into the far side—a fifty-pound weight on his chest as he lay back until his head touched the ground, then back up.

By the fourth complete rep his mind finally cleared enough that he could review what had happened.

Cindy had thrown him out. Only one word, "Leave!" and her own pointing finger jammed in the direction of the door.

Like the dog he was, he'd tucked his tail and run.

But it didn't make any sense. How was he supposed to know that Jimmy liked guys? Or liked him…that way? He knew it happened. This was the new, enlightened military. And that and ten cents didn't buy you a stick of gum. There was another stupid phrase. Had anyone ever sold gum by the stick? Must have, he supposed. But enlightened military? Yeah, right. No wonder Jimmy had gone so kick-ass tough.

Deek knocked back a bottle of water and went back to flipping the tractor tire up and down the brown packed-dirt stretch behind Task Command's CLUs. The containerized living units rose three stories high and were exclusively for the use of Special Operations teams. His present home, as much as he ever had one, was third row, second tier, fourth from the left.

Here behind the last row, the waste heat of all the individual air conditioners raised the temperature another five or ten degrees but at least they put out some damned moisture into the air, a few extra percent anyway. It also had the advantage of isolation. No one except security patrols wandered back here because the security fence which cut off the SOF compound from the rest of the camp stood only a few meters away. Any grunts out in the main camp wanted to watch him flip a tire, they were welcome to—he had nothing to do with them.

Deek supposed that Jimmy's actions made some kind of sense. Deek had never seen him with a girl. But then again…the three of them were total loners in high school. Deek still had been until Jimmy was assigned to his detail. He didn't know about Cindy, but there hadn't been a single picture in her office other than the Command-in-Chief's, such as it was.

Jimmy had always hung close to Deek when he had a chance. On the long quiet watches, he'd act as if he had something to say, but never did. And now Deek knew what it was.

Poor kid.

But that still didn't explain Cindy's reaction, sending him off like that.

His ears were starting to ring from the repeated thumps of the big tire on the hard earth. His muscles were well past burn and deep into sear. It felt good. It felt familiar. Another couple full reps and he'd go down to the rifle range to work on his accuracy while going through lactic acid withdrawal. He drank back half a bottle of water, dumped the rest on his head, turning the dust that coated him into mud, then chucked it aside and picked up the fifty pound weight.

Cindy had looked really pissed. Like some goddess of fury come to life. And he still didn't know why.

"You're a smart guy, Deek," he lay back then grunted himself upward to start another set of deep crunches with the weight on his chest.

"Figure it out." Crunch.

"She's mad because…" That lasted him through five more crunches without finding the next word.

"She's mad because…" he grunted upward again and froze.

Cindy was standing not ten feet away. Feet planted, arms crossed.

The fifty-pound weight he'd been clutching to his chest overbalanced him and took him down again. Coming back up from that one was hard. Once he was back up, he dumped the weight to the side and just looked at her.

She still looked absolutely amazing. Not the most beautiful girl in any crowd, but when you knew the person inside…nobody else stood a chance.

And he was sweaty, muddy, probably stank like a workout, and his breathing was so ragged that he was getting lightheaded just watching her.

Cindy stepped forward and, after he pulled in his legs, stepped into the tire and sat across the circle from him. Their knees were only inches apart. He leaned over for another two liter water bottle and their knees brushed together. He pulled his in closer and she did the same.

Guzzling down half the water did nothing for his parched throat.

"She…doesn't know why she's so mad," Cindy finally said softly.

"Huh." Deek couldn't think of anything else to say.

6

It was all jumbled up inside her. She had tried going back to her data, but it was a low priority research project that she still had a couple days on before it was needed. It hadn't been enough to draw her focus. Cindy had thought about going for a run…and had come to half an hour later still staring at her locked computer screen.

There was no way she could eat.

She didn't have any really close friends on base, didn't have any that she could call either. It was like when she found out her brother had died. No one to tell. No one to care.

Except for the man sitting across from her.

He hadn't been hard to find. She'd just followed the tortured grunts of someone working past their limits, but of course not acknowledging they had any limits to begin with. Nothing ever stopped Deek. Nothing.

"I didn't know," he finally said softly. "I swear I didn't."

"Neither did I."

He narrowed his eyes at her.

"I knew about Jimmy," her voice drifted softer. "I didn't know about you."

He nodded.

But there was more. Her assumptions weren't the only reason she hadn't tried to crack Derek Davies's loner shell. Who could want a girl who had chosen to be raped by her father? Even if it was to protect her brother. Nobody. That's who. Certainly not the only person she'd ever told about it. Jimmy had to know, to have understood. But he'd never let on. Some things were better never spoken about.

Whereas Deek…

"Oh my god. You're the one who stopped him."

"Your dad? Damn straight."

That took a second to sink in. Another thing she'd never known. Derek—Deek no longer sounded right to her—had protected both her and her brother. She covered her face for a long moment. How could she not have known? It was so obvious now that she thought about. "Friends" had been too strong a word for what they were, but they were *all* each other had in those times. She looked back up at him, unsure of what she'd see. But he still looked like the same, dirty, sweaty, amazing man he'd always been. Maybe a *lot* dirtier and sweatier than usual.

He shrugged his shoulders, not in a denying way, but rather as if he wished he could do it again. In retrospect she was surprised that Derek hadn't killed him outright. He'd certainly had the strength to.

"The photograph. That day." She'd never connected that either. "That was the day it all stopped."

He nodded and drank some more water.

"You said it was a day of celebration. That's why you smiled like that."

He looked aside for a long moment. "I did that for Jimmy. So that he'd know it was over. It was harder on him than you. He was never half as strong as you are. Maybe that's what made him try so hard as a Ranger, trying to make up for what he couldn't do as a kid. I was trying to cheer him up."

"Whereas me…"

Again, the look aside.

This time she waited him out.

He finally looked back. "You I held. Even for that one moment, I just held you safe."

She didn't know what to say and didn't have the chance.

"I also wanted to feel how someone could be so strong. Could take so much shit and still be so incredible. I wanted to know what it felt like to be as good as you. And care about someone, *anyone,* as much as you did for Jimmy. That caring was never part of my life, but it shone out of you like the sun. I've spent every minute since trying to live up to that feeling."

Cindy laughed, "I think that's the longest speech of your entire life."

Derek shrugged, finished the water, and smiled at her. Not grinned, smiled. Not the goofy look he'd made for her brother's sake. This was genuine and deep.

"I'm not all that strong."

"Bullshit!" Now Derek grinned. "Ain't a heroine in the movies got an edge on you. They're strong on the outside. Hell, any idiot can do that."

He thumped a fist against the tire and she could feel the vibration of it through her tailbone.

"You've got it in here."

He tapped her chest—they were close enough for that to be easy, though he pulled back his hand quickly and might even have blushed a little.

"That's how I made Delta. Trying to be as strong as you on the *inside*."

Cindy's head was spinning. One of America's top warriors, trying to be as strong as her. As he imagined her. No, as he *believed* her to be.

The way Derek saw her was…incredible.

"I told myself I was angry at you for rejecting Jimmy. For not returning what he felt so deeply for you."

Her man of few words was back, twisting his neck until she could practically hear the crackle along his spine.

"And I know for a fact that I was angry as hell that he got you and I didn't."

"But—"

"Shut up, Derek." The name felt like a caress as she said it. As if she could finally acknowledge the man, rather than the boy she kept at a careful distance.

He shut up.

"I wish to god I could tell Jimmy that. Not that I ever let him see it. But I wish I could tell him that and let him know I'm not angry at him any more."

"You were the one thing Jimmy and I always agreed on." Derek nodded as if talking to her brother right there, next around the circle on their tractor tire.

"What was that?"

"That you were the best woman on the planet."

"And you were both deluding yourselves." She wasn't any of that.

"Says you," again Derek smiled at her…for her…*because* of her. "From where I'm sitting," he thumped the tire again, "Jimmy and I had it dead to rights. Besides…"

He trailed off, then reached out to caress

her cheek. This time she let him and could feel that impenetrable wall she'd built so high—so high that she barely knew herself—simply get brushed aside as if it had never been there.

"Besides," he repeated in a whisper as soft as his caress. "It's rude to argue with both a dead man and the man who loves you."

He pulled her in, with the lightest of pressure.

Derek leaned in to meet her halfway, but paused just before their lips touched, when she could see herself so clearly in his dark eyes. "There's only ever been you, Cindy."

She swallowed against the tears, the tears that hadn't spilled at Jimmy's death, that hadn't spilled since she was a little girl afraid in the dark.

She was no longer afraid. Could never be with Derek beside her.

"There's only ever been you, Derek," she whispered back as the tears flowed.

Who knew that all of the tears stored inside her heart were tears of joy.

About the Author

M. L. Buchman has over 40 novels in print. His military romantic suspense books have been named Barnes & Noble and NPR "Top 5 of the year" and *Booklist* "Top 10 of the Year." He has been nominated for the Reviewer's Choice Award for "Top 10 Romantic Suspense of 2014" by *RT Book Reviews* and the prestigous RWA RITA Award in 2016. In addition to romance, he also writes thrillers, fantasy, and science fiction.

In among his career as a corporate project manager he has: rebuilt and single-handed a fifty-foot sailboat, both flown and jumped out of airplanes, designed and built two houses, and bicycled solo around the world.

He is now making his living as a full-time writer on the Oregon Coast with his beloved wife. He is constantly amazed at what you can do with a degree in Geophysics. You may keep up with his writing and receive free extras by subscribing to his newsletter at www.mlbuchman.com.

Target Engaged (excerpt)
-a Delta Force novel-

Carla Anderson rolled up to the looming, storm-fence gate on her brother's midnight-blue Kawasaki Ninja 1000 motorcycle. The pounding of the engine against her sore butt emphasized every mile from Fort Carson in Pueblo, Colorado, home of the 4th Infantry and hopefully never again the home of

Sergeant Carla Anderson. The bike was all she had left of Clay, other than a folded flag, and she was here to honor that.

If this was the correct "here."

A small guard post stood by the gate into a broad, dusty compound. It looked deserted and she didn't see even a camera.

This *was* Fort Bragg, North Carolina. She knew that much. Two hundred and fifty square miles of military installation, not counting the addition of the neighboring Pope Army Airfield.

She'd gotten her Airborne parachute training here and had never even known what was hidden in this remote corner. Bragg was exactly the sort of place where a tiny, elite unit of the U.S. military could disappear—in plain sight.

This back corner of the home of the 82nd Airborne was harder to find than it looked. What she could see of the compound through the fence definitely ranked "worst on base."

The setup was totally whacked.

Standing outside the fence at the guard post she could see a large, squat building across the compound. The gray concrete building was incongruously cheerful with bright pink roses along the front walkway—the only landscaping visible anywhere. More recent buildings—in better condition only because they were newer—ranged off to the right. She could breach the old fence in a dozen different places just in the hundred-yard span she could see before it disappeared into a clump of scrub and low trees drooping in the June heat.

Wholly indefensible.

There was no way that this could be the headquarters of the top combat unit in any country's military.

Unless this really was their home, in which case the indefensible fence—inde-fence-ible?—was a complete sham designed to fool a sucker. She'd stick with the main gate.

She peeled off her helmet and scrubbed at her long brown hair to get some air back into her scalp. Guys always went gaga over her hair, which was a useful distraction at times. She always wore it as long as her successive commanders allowed. Pushing the limits was one of her personal life policies.

She couldn't help herself. When there was a limit, Carla always had to see just how far it could be nudged. Surprisingly far was usually the answer. Her hair had been at earlobe length in Basic. By the time she joined her first forward combat team, it brushed her jaw. Now it was down on her shoulders. It was actually something of a pain in the ass at this length— another couple inches before it could reliably ponytail—but she did like having the longest hair in the entire unit.

Carla called out a loud "Hello!" at the empty compound shimmering in the heat haze.

No response.

Using her boot in case the tall chain-link fence was electrified, she gave it a hard shake, making it rattle loudly in the dead air. Not even any birdsong in the oppressive midday heat.

A rangy man in his late forties or early fifties, his hair half gone to gray, wandered around from behind a small shack as if he just happened to be there by chance. He was dressed like any off-duty soldier: worn khaki pants, a black T-shirt, and scuffed Army boots. He slouched to a stop and tipped his head to study her from behind his Ray-Bans. He needed a haircut and a shave. This was not a soldier out to make a good first impression.

"Don't y'all get hot in that gear?" He nodded

to indicate her riding leathers without raking his eyes down her frame, which was unusual and appreciated.

"Only on warm days," she answered him. It was June in North Carolina. The temperature had crossed ninety hours ago and the air was humid enough to swim in, but complaining never got you anywhere.

"What do you need?"

So much for the pleasantries. "Looking for Delta."

"Never heard of it," the man replied with a negligent shrug. But something about how he did it told her she was in the right place.

"Combat Applications Group?" Delta Force had many names, and they certainly lived to "apply combat" to a situation. No one on the planet did it better.

His next shrug was eloquent.

Delta Lesson One: *Folks on the inside of the wire didn't call it Delta Force. It was CAG or "The Unit."* She got it. Check. Still easier to think of it as Delta though.

She pulled out her orders and held them up. "Received a set of these. Says to show up here today."

"Let me see that."

"Let me through the gate and you can look at it as long as you want."

"Sass!" He made it an accusation.

"Nope. I just don't want them getting damaged or lost maybe by accident." She offered her blandest smile with that.

"They're that important to you, girlie?"

"Yep!"

He cracked what might have been the start of a grin, but it didn't get far on that grim face. Then he opened the gate and she idled the bike forward, scuffing her boots through the dust.

From this side she could see that the chain link was wholly intact. There was a five-meter swath of scorched earth inside the fence line. Through the heat haze, she could see both infrared and laser spy eyes down the length of the wire. And that was only the defenses she could see. So...a very *not* inde-fence-ible fence. Absolutely the right place.

When she went to hold out the orders, he waved them aside.

"Don't you want to see them?" This had to be the right place. She was the first woman in history to walk through The Unit's gates by order. A part of her wanted the man to acknowledge that. Any man. A Marine Corps marching band wouldn't have been out of order.

She wanted to stand again as she had on that very first day, raising her right hand. "I, Carla Anderson, do solemnly swear that I will support and defend the Constitution…"

She shoved that aside. The only man's acknowledgment she'd ever cared about was her big brother's, and he was gone.

The man just turned away and spoke to her over his shoulder as he closed the gate behind her bike. "Go ahead and check in. You're one of the last to arrive. We start in a couple hours"—as if it were a blasted dinner party. "And I already saw those orders when I signed them. Now put them away before someone else sees them and thinks you're still a soldier." He walked away.

She watched the man's retreating back. *He'd* signed her orders?

That was the notoriously hard-ass Colonel Charlie Brighton?

What the hell was the leader of the U.S. Army's Tier One asset doing manning the gate? Duh…assessing new applicants.

This place *was* whacked. Totally!

There were only three Tier One assets in the entire U.S. military. There was Navy's Special Warfare Development Group, DEVGRU, that the public thought was called SEAL Team Six—although it hadn't been named that for thirty years now. There was the Air Force's 24th STS—which pretty much no one on the outside had ever heard of. And there was the 1st Special Forces Operational Detachment—Delta—whose very existence was still denied by the Pentagon despite four decades of operations, several books, and a couple of seriously off-the-mark movies that were still fun to watch because Chuck Norris kicked ass even under the stupidest of circumstances.

Total Tier One women across all three teams? Zero.

About to be? One. Staff Sergeant First Class Carla Anderson.

Where did she need to go to check in? There was no signage. No drill sergeant hovering. No—

Delta Lesson Number Two: *You aren't in the Army anymore, sister.*

No longer a soldier, as the Colonel had

said, at least not while on The Unit's side of the fence. On this side they weren't regular Army; they were "other."

If that meant she had to take care of herself, well, that was a lesson she'd learned long ago. Against stereotype, her well-bred, East Coast white-guy dad was the drunk. Her dirt-poor half Tennessee Cherokee, half Colorado settler mom, who'd passed her dusky skin and dark hair on to her daughter, had been a sober and serious woman. She'd also been a casualty of an Afghanistan dust-bowl IED while serving in the National Guard. Carla's big brother Clay now lay beside Mom in Arlington National Cemetery. Dead from a training accident. Except your average training accident didn't include a posthumous rank bump, a medal, and coming home in a sealed box reportedly with no face.

Clay had flown helicopters in the Army's 160th SOAR with the famous Majors Beale and Henderson. Well, famous in the world of people who'd flown with the Special Operations Aviation Regiment, or their little sisters who'd begged for stories of them whenever big brothers were home on leave. Otherwise totally invisible.

Clay had clearly died on a black op that she'd never be told a word of, so she didn't bother asking. Which was okay. He knew the risks, just as Mom had. Just as she herself had when she'd signed up the day of Clay's funeral, four years ago. She'd been on the front lines ever since and so far lived to tell about it.

Carla popped Clay's Ninja—which is how she still thought of it, even after riding it for four years—back into first and rolled it slowly up to the building with the pink roses. As good a place to start as any.

***

"Hey, check out this shit!"

Sergeant First Class Kyle Reeves looked out the window of the mess hall at the guy's call. Sergeant Ralph last-name-already-forgotten was 75th Rangers and too damn proud of it.

Though…damn! Ralphie was onto something.

Kyle would definitely check out *this shit*.

Babe on a hot bike, looking like she knew how to handle it.

Through the window, he inspected her lean length as she clambered off the machine.

Army boots. So call her five-eight, a hundred and thirty, and every part that wasn't amazing curves looked like serious muscle. Hair the color of lush, dark caramel brushed her shoulders but moved like the finest silk, her skin permanently the color of the darkest tan. Women in magazines didn't look that hot. Those women always looked anorexic to him anyway, even the pinup babes displayed on Hesco barriers at forward operating bases up in the Hindu Kush where he'd done too much of the last couple years.

This woman didn't look like that for a second. She looked powerful. And dangerous.

Her tight leathers revealed muscles made of pure soldier.

Ralph Something moseyed out of the mess-hall building where the hundred selectees were hanging out to await the start of the next testing class at sundown.

Well, Kyle sure wasn't going to pass up the opportunity for a closer look. Though seeing Ralph's attitude, Kyle hung back a bit so that he wouldn't be too closely associated with the dickhead.

Ralph had been spoiling for a fight ever

since he'd found out he was one of the least experienced guys to show up for Delta selection. He was from the 75th Ranger Regiment, but his deployments hadn't seen much action. Each of his attempts to brag for status had gotten him absolutely nowhere.

Most of the guys here were 75th Rangers, 82nd Airborne, or Green Beret Special Forces like himself. And most had seen a shitload of action because that was the nature of the world at the moment. There were a couple SEALs who hadn't made SEAL Team Six and probably weren't going to make Delta, a dude from the Secret Service Hostage Rescue Team who wasn't going to last a day no matter how good a shot he was, and two guys who were regular Army.

The question of the moment though, who was she?

Her biking leathers were high-end, sewn in a jagged lightning-bolt pattern of yellow on smoke gray. It made her look like she was racing at full tilt while standing still. He imagined her hunched over her midnight-blue machine and hustling down the road at her Ninja's top speed—which was north of 150.

He definitely had to see that one day.

Kyle blessed the inspiration on his last leave that had made him walk past the small Toyota pickup that had looked so practical and buy the wildfire-red Ducati Multistrada 1200 instead. Pity his bike was parked around the back of the barracks at the moment. Maybe they could do a little bonding over their rides. Her machine looked absolutely cherry.

Much like its rider.

Ralph walked right up to her with all his arrogant and stupid hanging out for everyone to see. The other soldiers began filtering outside to watch the show.

"Well, girlie, looks like you pulled into the wrong spot. This here is Delta territory."

Kyle thought about stopping Ralph, thought that someone should give the guy a good beating, but Dad had taught him control. He would take Ralph down if he got aggressive, but he really didn't want to be associated with the jerk, even by grabbing him back.

The woman turned to face them, then unzipped the front of her jacket in one of those long, slow movie moves. The sunlight shimmered across her hair as she gave it an "unthinking" toss. Wraparound dark glasses hid her eyes, adding to the mystery.

He could see what there was of Ralph's brain imploding from lack of blood. He felt the effect himself despite standing a half-dozen paces farther back.

She wasn't hot; she sizzled. Her parting leathers revealed an Army green T-shirt and proof that the very nice contours suggested by her outer gear were completely genuine. Her curves weren't big—she had a lean build—but they were as pure woman as her shoulders and legs were pure soldier.

"There's a man who called me 'girlie' earlier." Her voice was smooth and seductive, not low and throaty, but rich and filled with nuance.

She sounded like one of those people who could hypnotize a Cobra, either the snake or the attack helicopter.

"He's a bird colonel. He can call me that if he wants. You aren't nothing but meat walking on sacred ground and wishing he belonged."

Kyle nodded to himself. The "girlie" got it in one.

"*You*"—she jabbed a finger into Sergeant

Ralph Something's chest—"do not get 'girlie' privileges. *We* clear?"

"Oh, sweetheart, I can think of plenty of privileges that you'll want to be giving to—" His hand only made it halfway to stroking her hair.

If Kyle hadn't been Green Beret trained, he wouldn't have seen it because she moved so fast and clean.

"—*me!*" Ralph's voice shot upward on a sharp squeak.

The woman had Ralph's pinkie bent to the edge of dislocation and, before the man could react, had leveraged it behind his back and up-ward until old Ralph Something was perched on his toes trying to ease the pressure. With her free hand, she shoved against the middle of his back to send him stumbling out of con-trol into the concrete wall of the mess hall with a loud *clonk* when his head hit.

Minimum force, maximum result. The Unit's way.

She eased off on his finger and old Ralph dropped to the dirt like a sack of potatoes. He didn't move much.

"Oops." She turned to face the crowd that had gathered.

She didn't even have to say, "Anyone else?" Her look said plenty.

Kyle began to applaud. He wasn't the only one, but he was in the minority. Most of the guys were doing a wait and see.

A couple looked pissed.

Everyone knew that the Marines' combat training had graduated a few women, but that was just jarheads on the ground.

This was Delta. The Unit was Tier One. A Special Mission Unit. They were supposed to be the one true bastion of male dominance. No one had warned them that a woman was coming in.

Just one woman, Kyle thought. The first one. How exceptional did that make her? Pretty damn was his guess. Even if she didn't last the first day, still pretty damn. And damn pretty. He'd bet on dark eyes behind her wraparound shades. She didn't take them off, so it was a bet he'd have to settle later on.

A couple corpsmen came over and carted Ralph Something away even though he was already sitting up—just dazed with a bloody cut on his forehead.

The Deltas who'd come out to watch the

show from a few buildings down didn't say a word before going back to whatever they'd been doing.

Kyle made a bet with himself that Ralph Something wouldn't be showing up at sundown's first roll call. They'd just lost the first one of the class and the selection process hadn't even begun. Or maybe it just had.

"Where's check-in?" Her voice really was as lush as her hair, and it took Kyle a moment to focus on the actual words.

He pointed at the next building over and received a nod of thanks.

That made watching her walk away in those tight leathers strictly a bonus.

Available at fine retailers everywhere.

Other works by M.L. Buchman

SMOKEJUMPERS
Wildfire at Dawn
Wildfire at Larch Creek
Wildfire on the Skagit

Delta Force
Target Engaged
Heart Strike

Angelo's Hearth
Where Dreams are Born
Where Dreams Reside
Maria's Christmas Table
Where Dreams Unfold
Where Dreams Are Written

Eagle Cove
Return to Eagle Cove
Recipe for Eagle Cove
Longing for Eagle Cove
Keepsake for Eagle Cove

Deities Anonymous
Cookbook from Hell: Reheated
Saviors 101

Dead Chef Thrillers
Swap Out!
One Chef!
Two Chef!

SF/F Titles
Nara
Monk's Maze

The Me and Elsie Chronicles

Newsletter signup at:
www.mlbuchman.com

20572463R00044

Printed in Great Britain
by Amazon